THIS BOOK BELONGS TO

_____

Icon Publishing Limited
P. O. Box OD 972
Odorkor, Accra
Ghana
www.facebook.com/myicongh
www.twitter.com/myicongh
+233 (0)23 3505 055,

iconpublishingltd@gmail.com
iconpublishing@ymail.com
enquiries.icongh@gmail.com

Cover and Interior Design by iCON-gh +233 24 4890 432

ISBN:  978-9988-8566-9-4

## AFRICAN FOLKTALE SERIES

# THE BOY WHO CUT OFF THE ELEPHANT'S TAIL

### A GHANAIAN FOLKTALE

Narrated by
Kwame Insaidoo

*This folktale from Ghana shows the extent that Ghanaians will go to—even putting themselves in debt or inconveniencing themselves—to show respect to their dead.*

Long, long ago, in a small village there lived a wise old man and his three grown sons, who catered to his every wish and took great care of him. He loved them just as much as they loved him. When the old man was approaching his hundredth birthday, he summoned his children to his room, and told them, "I am grateful that almighty God has richly blessed me to live to be almost one hundred years. You know that at the present time I am sitting close to my grave, and at anytime God may call me back home; so I want to know how you will put me away."

The man's children were sad to hear their beloved father speak so bluntly about his impending death; but they knew the old man was facing the reality of

*The wise old man and his three grown sons*

life, so they each told him about their preparations to bid him farewell.

The oldest son vowed that he would put him away with diamond and gold decorated wreath, and the second son promised to pay for the entire cost of the funeral and all other incidental expenses. The youngest son, as emotional as he was and quite determined to outdo his brothers, vowed that he would bury his dear, beloved father with the tail of the queen of the elephants. In their culture, only mighty kings and wealthy people were buried with the tails of elephant queens.

As the father predicted, he eventually met his day, and the children began to make their final preparations to put their beloved father away. As promised, the eldest son paid for a beautiful gold-plated wreath with diamonds, and the second son paid all the expenses for the funeral celebration.

The youngest son had the most challenging responsibility—procuring the tail of the queen of all the elephants—so he began his quest to get the tail in time for the celebrations. All eyes in the village were set on him to see if he was just running his mouth or if he knew what he was talking about. He began his trip to get the tail by walking toward the forest region where many elephants grazed on trees and herbs and jumped in pools of standing water.

He came to a small hut inhabited by an old, gray eccentric witch with long ears. The old lady was surprised to see a human being in her hut and asked him why he had travelled to a place where no human was supposed to set foot. The young man replied:

*Our beloved father passed away peacefully*
*And to put him away in style, I was obligated by our customs*
*To bring the family the tail of the queen of elephants*
*This symbolizes his high standing in our society*
*And so I am doomed if I do not bring the queen's tail*

The old witch told him that if the elephants were to see him, they would kill him instantly, but she was willing to help him because she admired his golden heart, which desired to help put his father away in a manner befitting a lovable and kindhearted parent. The old witch further informed him that the elephants were her friends and came to her daily with their queen and king to visit.

The witch continued, "The elephants and their queen will be here soon, and they will kill you if they find you

4

here, so I have to hide you in the little cave under my bedroom, which is not known to them."

She fed the boy and then hid him in the little cave under her bedroom. No sooner had the boy been tucked away in the cave than the elephants and their queen descended upon the old witch's hut. Immediately they all began to complain bitterly, "Old mama, we smell a strange human scent here. We have never smelled such a strong human scent before; we know that there is a human being here."

The elephants kept sniffing around the hut, the backyard, and the bedroom, but they could not see any human being. They remained disappointed and angry about the presence of the foul human scent, but the old witch put them at ease by reminding them, "I have been with you for many, many years and knew many of you when you were just born. If after all my help over the years, you are now tired of me and begin to call me human, and if my human scent now annoys you, then I am at your mercy. Kill me now that you are tired of me."

The elephants were apologetic to their old witch, and they all burst out, "We still love you, mama, and we will continue to love you till the end of time."

The elephants ate their food and talked with the old witch for some time and then left for the night. The witch waited for an hour before bringing the boy out of the cave. She gave him a sharp knife and asked him to listen closely to what she had to say.

The old witch instructed him as follows: "Elephants are powerful animals, and any little deviation from my instructions will result in your death. They will pounce on you and eat you up, so what you need to do is wait in the valley till you hear them snoring and making their peculiar sound, 'Wheeto, wheeto, wheeto.' But if you hear them making another noise, 'Hurutu, hurutu, hurutu' that means they are not asleep, only talking to each other. If you dare go near them then, they will eat you up. Make sure to pay attention until you hear the snoring sounds only. Finally, the queen of all the elephants is jet-black and sleeps in the last row of all the elephants. You must walk firmly across all the elephants until you get to the last one; then cut her tail off and run quickly back to me."

The young boy thanked the old witch and left her little hut with the large knife, ready to follow exactly what he was told to do. He quietly hid in the hill overlooking the valley where the elephants slept, and waited. But as he waited, he continued to hear *"hurutu, hurutu, hurutu"* and knew that the elephants were not asleep, so he lay low until he heard the peculiar snoring sounds, *"wheeto, wheeto, wheeto."* Then he knew that the elephants were asleep.

He looked all around where he was hiding but saw nothing, so he mustered all the strength and courage he could, marched boldly and swiftly across the tops of the elephants until he came face-to-face with the queen of the elephants, lying there in her splendour and majesty with jet-black skin. His heart was trembling with fear, but he summoned his courage and willpower, and despite being as fearful as he was, he swiftly slashed off the tail of the queen and ran as quickly as he could back to the old lady's hut.

The old witch congratulated him for following her instructions and successfully obtaining the tail of the queen of the elephants, but she warned him to be careful in all his undertaking and never speak to strangers about what had happened that night. Furthermore, the witch gave him a mirror to keep with him at all times and look into periodically to see what the elephants were doing—playing, fighting, or attempting to come after him for cutting off the tail of their queen.

The young boy graciously thanked the old witch and frantically left the hut with the tail of the elephant queen tucked in a sack. When he left the old witch's hut he ran as fast as his legs could carry him through the grasslands and forests, crossing many streams and struggling to get to the funeral celebration of his dear father.

Meanwhile, the chief priest of the elephant woke up in the middle of the night and exclaimed with a shrill voice that woke up all the elephants, "I had an awful nightmare that the tail of our queen was cut off by an intruder."

The elephants jumped up in excitement and rushed to the side of the queen, and indeed her tail had been cut off. There was a pandemonium in the elephant valley, and in their anger, they stampeded to the old witch's hut and complained to her that they had been right about their suspicions of a human presence near her house.

"A human has chopped off the tail of our dear beloved queen!" they exclaimed. The old witch pretended not to know what they were saying and told them to go look for their human and do whatever they wanted with him.

The angry elephants stampeded along the road, making shrill noises, determined to catch and kill the human who had succeeded in wickedly cutting off the tail of their queen. The elephants raced through the forests and grasslands and crossed all the streams and rivers in the jungle but could not get the boy. The elephants gave up the chase for the time being, but the queen decided on a different strategy to get the boy.

The young boy returned to the village in the midst of the festivities and waved the tail of the queen of the elephants to the well-wishers and the mourners. The village erupted with shouts, as people congratulated him and lifted him high up in the sky for his great accomplishments. The young man had made his father proud by burying him with the elephant queen's tail and bestowing upon him the dignity reserved only for kings and other high dignitaries. The young man's fame spread all over the towns and villages in the area, where he was praised for his greatness, courage, and audacity.

Long after the funeral celebrations, the queen of the elephants transformed herself into a beautiful, shapely lady dressed in expensive Kente cloth and trekked to the village where the young man who had cut off her tail lived.

When she got to the middle of the town, she sat under a big tree and spread gold earrings, necklaces, and other ornaments on the ground, pretending that she was selling them. She tied a thin thread from one end of a branch to the other end and challenged that she would marry the skilled person who could strike the thin thread with an arrow. Many of the bachelors in the village tried to strike the thread, but none could. Even the disabled and blind men attempted to strike the thread with their arrows but could not.

One of the onlookers was disgusted that none of the men in the village could strike the thread, and he frowned upon them and said, "I know the young man who buried his father with the tail of the queen of the elephants could easily pierce this stupid thread with his bow and arrow."

The beautiful lady responded, "Well, I doubt if that young man has the dexterity and the wherewithal to successfully strike this thin thread, but if he succeeds, I will promptly marry him."

The onlooker wanted to show the stranger that he knew what he was talking about, so he rushed to fetch the young man, who was busy hunting lions and tigers.

When the young man heard the challenge, he laughed and promptly went to see the lady under the tree to hear what the challenge was all about. He laughed uproariously when he saw the thread, and he bragged to the multitude of onlookers and all the bachelors who had already failed to strike the thread that he could easily complete the task.

"So, none of you has been able to strike this thread? Don't you all know me as the champion who cut off the tail of the queen of the elephants to bury with my late father?" He continued to brag, "I hunt for lions, tigers, and elephants, not silly threads. I will destroy this one in the twinkling of an eye."

The queen of the elephants was filled with rage inside and was disgusted at the bravado of the little boy. She vowed to tear him into pieces when she got the chance. Everybody looked on and cheered as the young man shot his arrow and struck the middle of the thread, tearing it into two. The villagers clapped

*Onlookers cheering the young man as he shot his arrow and*
*struck the middle of the thread, tearing it into two.*

and clapped for the young man for successfully doing what no others in the village could do.

The beautiful lady responded, "You are not the man I was expecting, but it seems fate has put our lives together and we have no choice but to be together for what all that entails."

The young man considered himself lucky to get the chance to marry such a beautiful lady, but he did not know that he was about to marry his worst enemy, who was secretly determined to destroy him. The young man and the strange lady were married by the village chief, and they moved into the young man's hut.

At night when they went to bed, the beautiful lady turned into the jet black elephant queen and chased her husband all around the room, attempting to kill him, but the young man used his magic and clapped his hands to turn himself into a pillow. The elephant searched frantically for her husband but could not find him. As usual she was furious and swore that, when she got hold of him, she would destroy him.

The next day when they woke up, neither said anything to the other, but they instinctively knew that the battle lines were drawn between them. The young man realized by then that he had married his worst and sworn enemy and therefore had to be extremely careful if he was to survive at all.

The young man told his wife to join him on his farm late in the morning and to bring him his lunch. Then he left for his farm. When he arrived, he wrapped his magic potion in a leaf and hid it in the trunk of large oak tree. Unfortunately for him when his wife reached the farm, she went straight to the trunk of the tree and set his magic on fire. Then she turned into an elephant and began chasing him all over the farm. She made a loud, shrill sound that called the rest of the elephants to her, and they all began chasing after him, with the intent of tearing him into little pieces.

When the young boy clapped, his magic potion responded, "Help yourself, because I am burning up and cannot help you."

When all the elephants closed in on him, the black queen lifted her tusks, ready to plunge them into his heart, but the young man frantically screamed and called on his magic again. Immediately, he turned into a bird and flew away.

Moral Lessons

This tale has many lessons for all of us to consider. First we see that the young man was persistent and courageous in struggling to accomplish the nearly impossible feat of procuring the tail of the queen of the elephants to bury with his respected and admirable father. Additionally, we learn a valuable lesson about marriages; it was unwise for the young man to marry a total stranger. He never bothered to learn more about her: where she came from or her motivation for hanging the thread, looking for bachelors to pierce the arrow, and offering to marry the winner.

The young man could and should have asked himself many critical questions before foolishly plunging into the marriage with a total stranger: Why had she selected his village despite the fact that there were many other villages in the area? Who sent her to his village? Why was such a beautiful person not married already? Why was she looking for strangers to marry? What type of lady was she and what was she running away from to marry in a distant village? Who were her parents, siblings, and friends? The lesson here is that before marrying somebody we should find out more about them.

.....................................

Congratulations! We know you enjoyed reading. Now, go ahead and attempt answering the following questions:

1.  a) How did the three grown sons treat their wise old father?

    b) What was the father's message when he summoned the three children to his room?

2.  What did each of the children vow towards bidding their father farewell after his demise?

3.  a) What were the old witch's instructions to the boy?

    b) What happened after the old witch fed the boy and then hid him in the little cave under her bedroom?

4.  a) How did the old witch prepare the boy for the final hunt?

b) How successful was the boy in his quest for the queen of the elephants' tail?

c) What did the angry elephants do in the middle of the night?

5. In the midst of the festivities, how did the villagers welcome the young boy?

6. What challenge did the 'beautiful lady' put before the villagers?

7. a) On the night of their marriage, what saved the young man from being destroyed by the queen of the elephants?

b) How did the young man survive the elephants attack on the farm the following day?

8. What have you learned from this folktale?

9. Find the meaning of the following words in the dictionary and use them in sentences of your own,

i. Summoned

ii. Bluntly

iii. Impending

iv. Wreath

v. Affluent

vi. Procuring

vii. Eccentric

Answer the questions here.